Masha and the Bear

For Freya. Enjoy reading books on your own! — L. D.

For Evie . . . Lots of love, Auntie Mels x — M. W.

Barefoot Books
2067 Massachusetts Ave
Cambridge, MA 02140

Series Editor: Gina Nuttall
Text copyright © 2013 by Lari Don
Illustrations copyright © 2013 by Melanie Williamson
The moral rights of Lari Don and Melanie Williamson have been asserted

Graphic design by Penny Lamprell, Hampshire, UK
Color separation by B & P International, Hong Kong
Printed in China on 100% acid-free paper
This book was typeset in Tractor, Classy Diner and Bembo Infant
The illustrations were prepared in acrylic, pencil and chalk

Thank you to Y2 at St. Anne's Catholic Primary School, Caversham, UK
for all their careful reading

Sources:
Riordan, James. "Little Masha and Misha the Bear" in *Tales from Central Russia*.
Viking Children's Books, New York, 1976.

ISBN 978-1-84686-874-0

Library of Congress Cataloging-in-Publication Data is available under
LCCN 2012035927

1 3 5 7 9 8 6 4 2

Masha and the Bear

A Story from Russia

Retold by Lari Don • Illustrated by Melanie Williamson

Barefoot Books
step inside a story

Contents

CHAPTER 1

A Basket of Berries

Once upon a time, there was a little girl called Masha. She was picking berries in the forest. She stayed on the edge of the forest so she could see her house.

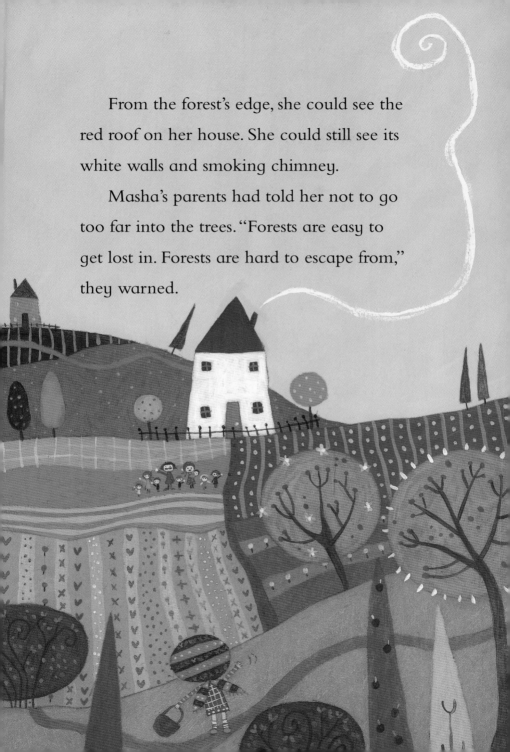

From the forest's edge, she could see the red roof on her house. She could still see its white walls and smoking chimney.

Masha's parents had told her not to go too far into the trees. "Forests are easy to get lost in. Forests are hard to escape from," they warned.

Soon Masha had picked all the ripe
fruit on the bushes at the edge of the forest.
But Masha's basket was not full and she
had lots of brothers and sisters to feed.

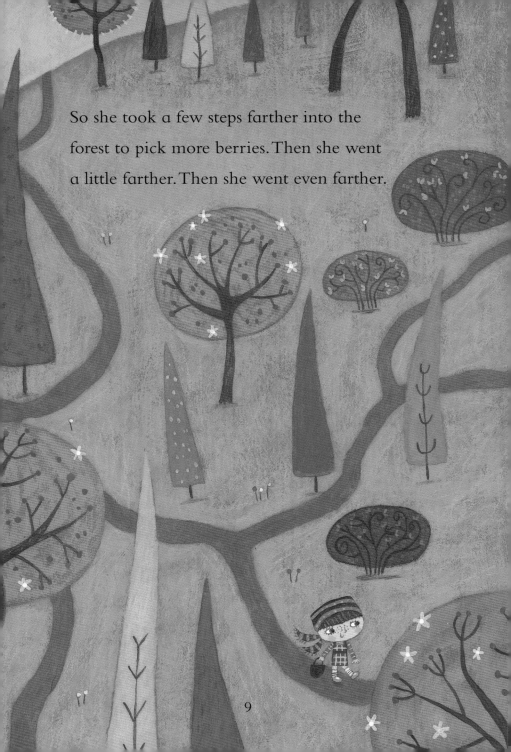

So she took a few steps farther into the
forest to pick more berries. Then she went
a little farther. Then she went even farther.

Now her basket was full. She turned
around to go home. But she could not
see the red roof or the white walls of her
house. She could not smell the sweet wood
smoke from the chimney. Masha did not
know which way to go. She was lost!

CHAPTER 2

Lost!

Masha went left. Then she went right.
She looked all around. But she could not
see the edge of the forest. She could not see
her house. Masha was scared.

And she was not alone.

Something was watching her from
behind a tree. It was a big brown bear.
The bear stepped out and padded toward
Masha. He said in a gruff voice, "Are you
lost, little girl?"

"Yes, Mr. Bear," replied Masha.

"Do you want to go home?" asked
the bear.

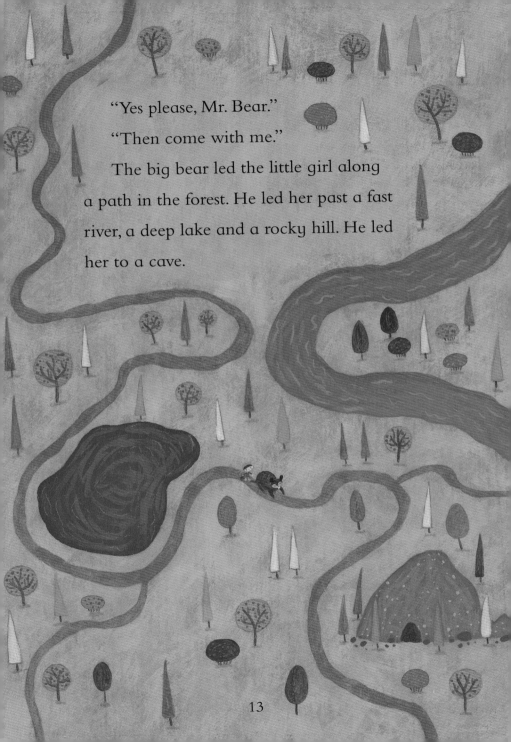

"Yes please, Mr. Bear."

"Then come with me."

The big bear led the little girl along a path in the forest. He led her past a fast river, a deep lake and a rocky hill. He led her to a cave.

Masha said, "But this is a cave! This is not my home!"

"No," laughed the bear. "This is my home!"

CHAPTER 3

The Bear's Cave

It was cold and lonely in the forest,
so Masha went into the bear's cave. She
shared her basket of berries with the bear.
She chatted with him about her lovely home.

She told the bear about its red roof and its white walls. She talked about the smell of the sweet wood smoke. And she told him about the tasty pies she baked with fruit. Then she fell asleep.

The next morning, Masha said to the bear, "Can you take me home now?"

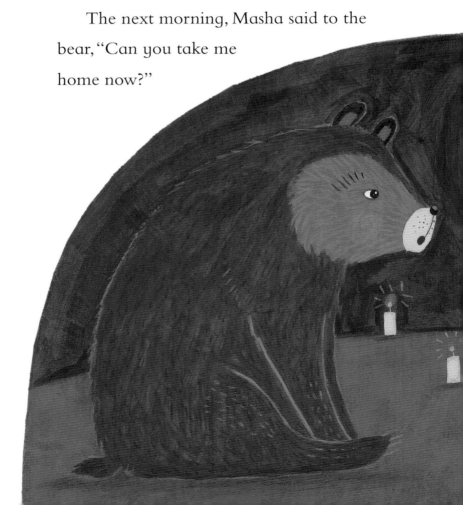

"No!" said the bear. "No. I want you to stay here and make my cave as lovely as your home. I want you to sweep the floor for me and light fires for me. I want you to cook pies for me."

He stood up and blocked the door of the dusty cave. He crossed his big, furry arms over his big, furry chest. He stayed there until Masha nodded.

She picked up a broom and started to sweep the floor.

Masha missed her home. She missed
her mother and her father. She missed her
sisters and even her brothers. But the bear
would not let her go far from the cave. And
he would never let her go home.

As Masha cleaned and swept and dusted and cooked, she came up with a clever plan.

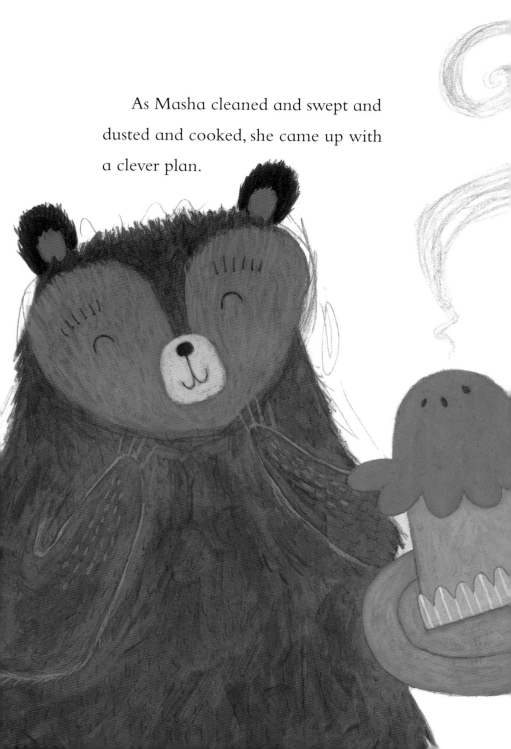

Instead of crying, she smiled at the bear. Instead of nagging to go home, she sang songs as she worked. Instead of moaning, she baked the best cakes and pies ever. So the bear grew very fond of her.

One day, Masha waited until the bear
had just eaten a big apple tart. He was full
and happy. He was rubbing his fat tummy.
Then she said, "Dearest Bear, can I ask
you a favor?"

"No," growled the bear. "No, Masha, I won't let you go home."

"I know that, dearest Bear. I am not asking to go home. But my family doesn't know where I am. I came into the forest to pick berries for them a long time ago, and they must be worried about me."

"Please can you take my family a gift from me?" Masha asked. "Then my family will know I am safe and happy here with you."

"Next time I bake you a big cherry
pie," Masha told the bear, "I will also bake
seven little cherry pies. I will bake four
for my brothers and three for my sisters. I
would be so happy if you would take the
little pies through the forest and leave them
at the gate for my family."

The bear wanted a happy, singing
Masha. He wanted her to stay and make
his home a cheerful place. So he agreed.

I agree.

CHAPTER 4

Masha's Plan

The next morning, Masha picked lots of ripe red cherries from the trees outside the cave. She rolled the pastry and baked the pies. She made one enormous pie for the bear. Then she made seven smaller pies for her brothers and sisters.

She chatted to the bear while she
baked. "Now, dearest Bear, I know you love
cherry pies. But these little pies are not for
you. They're for my brothers and sisters.
So please don't sit down and nibble a
cherry pie on the way to my house."

"Oh no, Masha, I won't," said the bear.

"Do you promise?" asked Masha.

"Yes, I promise," agreed the bear.

"I do believe you, dearest Bear, but I just want to be sure."

"When you have gone," Masha said, "I shall climb to the top of the tallest tree. From up there, I can keep an eye on you. I can make sure that the pies get to my family safely. And I can make sure that you get back home safely too."

30

Masha took the pies out of the oven and gave the big pie to the bear. While he was busy eating, she put four of the small pies into the basket, around the edge. Then she stepped into the basket herself.

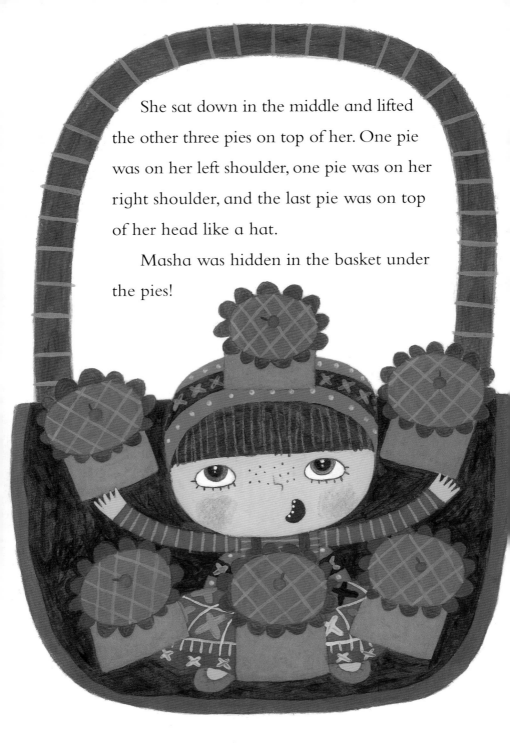

She sat down in the middle and lifted the other three pies on top of her. One pie was on her left shoulder, one pie was on her right shoulder, and the last pie was on top of her head like a hat.

Masha was hidden in the basket under the pies!

The bear picked up the basket and began to walk through the forest. When he reached the rocky hill, he stopped. He sat down because the basket was heavy. As he rested his paws, he thought about eating another cherry pie.

"They smell so good," he said to
himself. "Does Masha really have seven
brothers and sisters? Do they all need a pie?"

He put his big, furry paw into
the basket to pick up a cherry pie.
He wanted the cherry pie on the left.

"I See You, Bear!"

As the bear's paw curled around the cherry pie on top of Masha's left shoulder, Masha whispered, "I see you, Bear! I hope you aren't going to eat the pie I baked for my littlest sister!"

The bear quickly snatched back his
paw. He said, "That little girl has sharp
eyes to see me from so far away."

He picked up the basket and walked
on. When he reached the deep lake,
he stopped.

He sat down because the basket was
heavy. As he rested his paws, he thought
again about eating a cherry pie.

"They smell so good," he said. "I don't
think Masha's brothers and sisters need all
these pies. Why can't they share?"

He put his big, furry paw slowly into the basket to pick up a cherry pie. He wanted the cherry pie on top of Masha's right shoulder. His claws touched the pie crust!

Masha whispered, "I see you, Bear! I hope you aren't going to eat the pie I baked for my littlest brother!"

The bear quickly snatched back his paw. He said, "That little girl has a loud voice to carry all that way."

Oh!

He picked up the basket and walked
on. When he reached the bend in the river,
he stopped. He sat down because the
basket was heavy. As he rested his paws,
he thought again about eating another
cherry pie.

"They smell so good," he said to himself. "Perhaps not all her little brothers and sisters like cherries. I'm sure I can have just one."

He put his big, furry paw into the basket
to pick up a cherry pie. He wanted the cherry
pie that wobbled on top of Masha's head! He
hooked his claws under the pie dish.

CHAPTER 6

Home, Sweet Home

Masha whispered, "I see you, Bear!
I hope you aren't going to eat the pie I
baked for the new baby!"

The bear quickly snatched back his
paw. He said, "That little girl must be up a
very tall tree!"

The big brown bear picked up the basket and walked on. When he reached the edge of the forest, he stopped. He didn't like the wide open fields or the long roads. He didn't like the neat houses or the busy people.

But he was sure Masha was still watching him from the tallest tree.

He was sure she was ready to say, "I see
you, Bear!" So he padded out of the forest.
He walked up to the house with the red roof,
the white walls and the long line of sweet
smoke. He put the basket down at the gate.
Then he ran back to the forest.

When he was gone, Masha climbed out
of the basket and skipped into the house.
Masha's mother and father got their
little girl back. And Masha's brothers and
sisters got a cherry pie each! They all
smiled and laughed as they ate their pies.

And what happened to the big brown
bear? He had to learn to do all his own
cooking and cleaning. He had to learn
how to bake his own cherry pies!